Stock and Rocket

Published in 2018
by Stock and Rocket, an imprint of
Igloo Books Ltd, Cottage Farm
Sywell, NN6 0BJ
www.igloobooks.com

FIR003 1118
2 4 6 8 10 9 7 5 3 1
ISBN 978-1-78905-285-5

© iStock / Getty Images

Written by Elizabeth Dale
Illustrated by Paula Bowes

Printed and manufactured in China

This book belongs to:

. . . .

Ed the Explorer

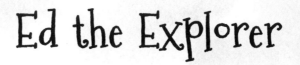

Ed the ted and his friend, Matt, loved playing explorers together in the garden. They found footprints in the mud, and dens under bushes. Nothing scared them, not even crocodiles in the pond.

"We are brave explorers off on an exciting adventure!" cried Matt, as he led the way with his stick. "Maybe we will even find a scary monster."

Suddenly, Matt saw a shadow behind the shed. "Shh! I think it's a monster."
Just then, Matt's mum called out. "Time for your dinner!" she said.
"Oh, no!" cried Matt. "Ed, you look for the monster and I'll come back later."

Ed was very excited as Matt ran inside. He'd never been on an adventure on his own before. He looked all around him, ready to spot the monster in case it appeared.

As Ed watched and waited, it soon began to get dark. HOOT! Ed jumped.
What was that? He looked all around him and saw something swoop low.
"Maybe it's the monster," said Ted, but it was just an owl.

As it grew darker, Ed heard
snuffling in the long grass.
"I think it's the monster,"
he said, quivering.

The sound was
getting louder and louder.
Suddenly, a rabbit
hopped by.

Ed didn't want to be an explorer all alone in the dark anymore.
"I want to go back inside," he said. Just then, he saw a shadow. It grew
bigger and came closer and closer. "It's the monster!" he cried.

"There you are, Ed," said a friendly voice. It was Matt.
He picked Ed up and gave him a big cuddle. "Come on," he said.
"That's enough exploring for today."

The Teddy Show

Teddy was excited, he was putting on a show.
All of his friends and family had told him they would go.

He practised some magic tricks. They were all very good.
Except the rabbits didn't appear exactly when they should.

Teddy tried his juggling tricks. He loved them best of all.
He did them standing on one leg and didn't drop one ball.

"I'll do a dance," Teddy said, as he danced and sang a song so sweet.
"The audience will love to see my magnificent dancing feet."

At last it was the big
show night and Teddy
was so thrilled.

He peeped around
the curtain to see
the hall was filled.

The show began and it went so well, the audience gave a cheer.
Then, Teddy reached inside his hat and made lots of rabbits appear.

Teddy did some juggling tricks and saved his dance until last.
Then, as he jumped, he tripped and fell and everybody gasped.

The crowd laughed and cheered. "He's funny, too!" they cried.
Instead of bursting into tears, Teddy beamed with pride.

This
Treasure Cove Story
belongs to

I AM SIMBA

A CENTUM BOOK 978-1-913265-94-6
Published in Great Britain by Centum Books Ltd.
This edition published 2020.

1 3 5 7 9 10 8 6 4 2

Centum Books Ltd, 20 Devon Square, Newton Abbot,
Devon, TQ12 2HR, UK.

www.centumbooksltd.co.uk | books@centumbooksltd.co.uk
CENTUM BOOKS Limited Reg. No. 07641486.

A CIP catalogue record for this book is available
from the British Library.

Printed in China.

centum

DISNEY

THE LION KING

I AM SIMBA

By John Sazaklis
Illustrated by Alan Batson

I am **SIMBA**.

I am a lion cub.

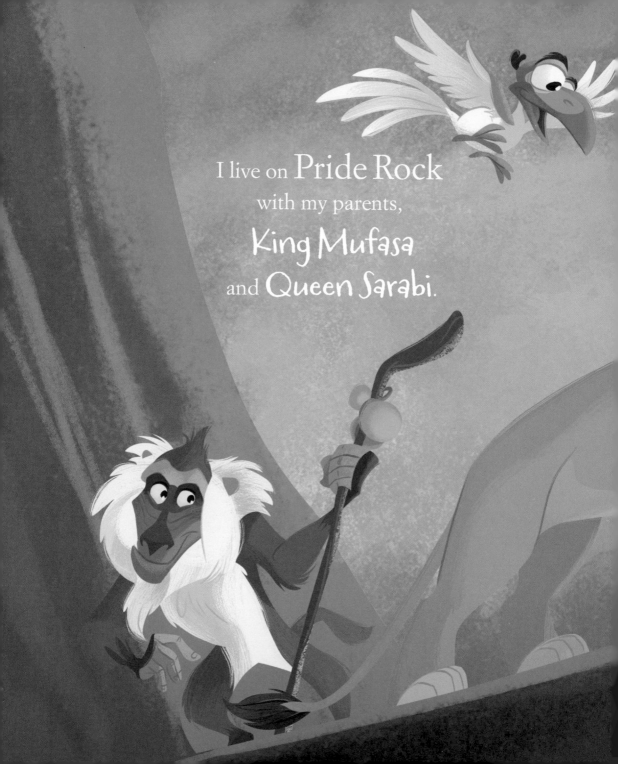

I live on Pride Rock
with my parents,
King Mufasa
and Queen Sarabi.

When I grow up, I'll
be in charge. I can't wait
to be **king**!

I don't always follow my father's rules.

Zazu the hornbill tries to keep me out of trouble.

Trouble is one way
to describe my uncle Scar.

He is mean and
hangs out with the
hyenas – they are
the sworn enemies
of Pride Rock!

I am brave.

I like to go on

ADVENTURES

with my best friend, Nala.

We sneak into the elephant graveyard.

Yikes! Hyenas!

I let out a

ROAR

to scare the hyenas, but they just laugh at me.

HA HA HA HAAAA

Scar tells me I must go away, so I run deep into the jungle.

There I meet Timon the meerkat and Pumbaa the warthog.

YUCK!

I am so hungry,
I could eat a whole zebra!
Timon and Pumbaa offer
me bugs instead.

My new best friends teach me a wonderful phrase: 'HAKUNA MATATA.' It means 'No worries.'

Years pass. I am no longer a little cub.

It was fun getting to play all day,
but I missed my old home.

While I was away, Nala grew up, too.
I am happy to see her again.

I learn that Pride Rock is
in trouble. Scar and the
hyenas are in charge!

It is my duty to make things right.
I ask Timon and Pumbaa to help.

We are best friends *fur*-ever!

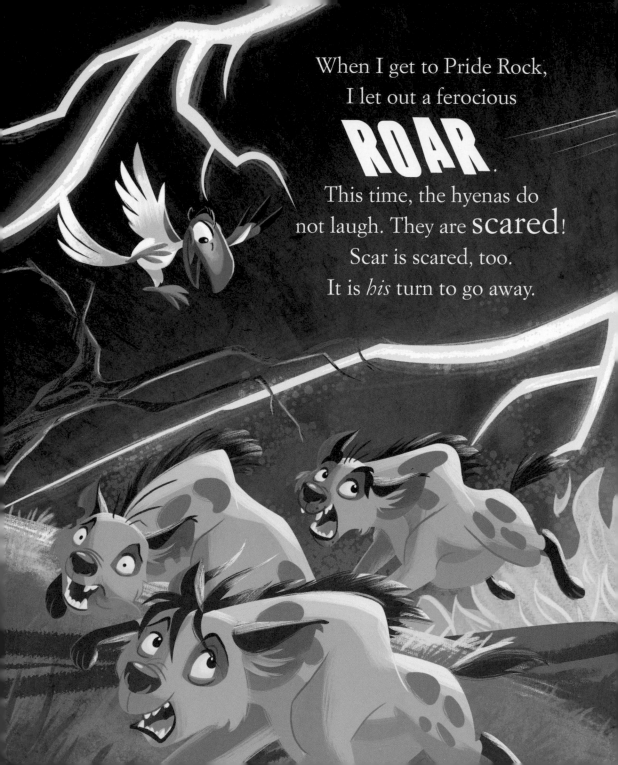

When I get to Pride Rock,
I let out a ferocious

ROAR.

This time, the hyenas do
not laugh. They are scared!
Scar is scared, too.
It is *his* turn to go away.

Now I am the **LION KING** and Nala is the queen.

We welcome our baby cub
into the
Circle of Life.

I am **SIMBA**,

and I am proud of my pride.

Treasure Cove Stories

Please contact Centum Books to receive the full list of titles in the *Treasure Cove Stories* series.
books@centumbooksltd.co.uk

Classic favourites

Recently published

Latest publications

Book list may be subject to change.